"WE ARE SURVIVORS" yelled the last of the resistance as they pushed back the Chinese army. The communist oppressors had riot shields and weapons but we did not relent. But I'm getting ahead of myself. Hi, my name is Michael. This all happened three years ago... This is my story.

Chapter One

Hi, I'm Michael Tanning; I'm 5'5 with dark hair and big brown eyes, which are generally covered by my dark hair.

Because of the leak of the names of some spies in China, there has been talk of invasions and war between the Chinese and us Americans. President Mark Lucas has addressed the situation and stressed that we all stay calm and continue with our everyday business. But how can you stay calm in a situation like this? Later that week, there was a war council in Washington D.C. to vote on how action should be taken and what procedure should be used. Although there were multiple attempts to rescue the remaining two of the seven under-cover spies hidden in China, they all failed. Finally, President Mark renamed the situation as "Terror Level 3," meaning that there is a chance of an invasion or war.

Over time, it got worse. My family and I would barely get any sleep during the week. My mother, Margarette, would take the first shift and wake us if there was anything important. Next would be my dad, Charles, with the same routine. My little brother, Zach, was the only one in the family who didn't have to worry about being up at odd hours, hoping that there was no siren or to hear the familiar and always scary sound of a helicopter or plane.

The next day after that, all guardians and people above 18 were called to city hall to be briefed on what should happen if we were invaded. Luckily, that didn't pertain to me, because I was only 16 years old. But still, the only possible thing that could calm me down was talking to Erin, my girlfriend. She is beautiful, with brown eyes and dark colored hair. She's shorter than I am, so I feel comfortable hugging or holding her. However, because of the time it takes to get there, her father doesn't agree with me coming all the way to the suburbs of Hinesville, Georgia, to see her. Gosh, I love her... but I'm getting ahead of myself again.

By now, my parents had returned. I recognized the worried look on my mother's face. "Michael, you and Zach go pack your bags," she said, as she tried to hold back the tears.

"Margarette, you're scaring them," my dad responded, as he gritted his teeth and tried to hold his lips together as he talked (much like a ventriloquist).

"Pack your bags!" my mother snapped.

With no questions asked, my little brother and I went upstairs.

"What do you think we're packing for?" My brother asked, clearly worried.

All I could think of to say was, "I don't know but hurry up."

Soon we were both down stairs with our bags in-hand. "Where are we going?" I asked impatiently.

By this time, both of my parents were in hysterics but my dad managed to choke out five words that changed my life forever. "We're not going, you are."

Chapter Two

After hearing the news, I sobbed, hard. My family and I gathered together. We cried and prayed for about an hour. We all knew that this was probably the last time that we'd ever see each other and we'd never see our parents again. We agreed to talk on the phone daily from the children's shelter.

A couple hours later, people came to our home to take us to the shelter. It took about 10 minutes to pull Zach away from my parents. The next thing I knew, I was in a tiny blue car with Zach looking out the window. We rode for what seemed to be an hour. At last, we arrived. It was a large building with many windows. It looked like a renovated Recreation Center.

When we went through the front door, we were greeted by loud noises and crying. The "nice" people who had come to take us away just put us in a large room, shut the door, and left.

"Hi," a girl said, as she walked beside us.

"Ummm, hey," I replied nervously. (Mostly because I didn't know what her intentions were.)

"I'm Marisa," she said, as she stretched out her hand.

Zach shook it and I pulled him behind me. "We're new," I said as I apologized for being so anti-social.

"Oh, so am I," she smiled, "I don't know where my little brother is, he's about the same size as your brother and he just turned seven."

"Hey, my brother's seven too," I said, as I smiled back. "Wanna help her find him?" I turned to ask Zach.

His eyes lit up and he went with her to help her find her brother. In the meantime, I scouted the building for a place to sleep. I found a small corner behind what seemed to be a playpen. Just as I put our belongings down, Marisa, Zach, and what seemed to be her brother walked through the crowd and to the corner. "Michael, this is Luke. Say 'hi' to Michael, Luke," she commanded and he obeyed.

It was obvious that he was either nervous or just shy by the scared look in his eyes, as if we were going to hurt him or take him away.

Just then, there was a loud bang and everyone got quiet. I'm guessing that everybody else had been there a while because they all knew what to do.

"It's 9:00!" Yelled a booming voice that came from multiple intercoms in every corner of the room. "Find a place to sleep and be quiet. That is all." Then the voice was quiet.

"It's already 9:00?" I asked confused. Just a couple of hours ago, I had been embracing my beautiful, teary-eyed, mother, and worrisome father. Just then, I noticed that I hadn't had anything to eat since then, but it didn't matter much at that point.

"Psst," whispered Marissa.

"Yea?" I replied.

She took a long pause, as she looked at me, and finally asked, "If the Chinese invade, we will stay here, you know that, right?"

The only thing that I could reply with was, "Yea."

"Do you want to stay and probably die here?" She asked, as she also held back tears.

"No, why are you asking?" Now, I was starting to get worried, because if she thinks we can survive out there by ourselves, she might be crazy.

"Let's break out." She replied.

Chapter Three

The next few weeks went by fast. I learned that about 80% of the people in there were "bad-apples" and I quickly learned how to protect all four of us at the same time. I also learned many skills, such as how to hot-wire a car and pick pockets. Because he was older and if we do have to break out, he'll be on our side; Marissa made good friends with the guy who taught me this. He was turning 18 next month and his name was Trae. He was about six feet tall and extremely muscular. I think he was the biggest person in there. He had black hair with grey eyes and a long face. His expression never changed, except when he fought. He had this look of joy when he used his fist or anything that required a thievish state of mind. We eventually gained his trust though and he slept in our corner with us. Everything was fine until midnight.

Chapter Four

I woke up to a faint repeating whistle. Over and over, I kept hearing the whistles. Then, out of nowhere, there was this loud, ear-splitting boom. Everyone awoke screaming and in distress. The familiar voice came on over the microphones, urging us to stay calm, and that it was just procedure. Nobody believed that.

Trae woke up Marisa, as I woke up Zach and Luke. We hurriedly emptied our bags and tied the sleeping bags that we had been issued.

In the hope of finding supplies, I immediately ran for the storage room, past the crying cloud. There was a small box labeled "emergency" on one of the shelves; I stuffed that in my bag, while looking around for anything that else that could be of use.

When I left that room, I ran into the rest of the group and we ran to a spare room that only Trae knew about. He opened the food that was to be used in case of fire and we made a break for it, not even looking back.

Chapter Five

We ran at a steady pace for what seemed to be miles. Then we were startled by planes and booming notices. To my left, I could see smoke, probably from fires caused by the explosions. We kept running. We ran until our legs caved in and broke down. Then we rested together at an old rickety building. There were sirens, gunshots, screams, and explosions all around us. I had completely forgotten about my parents, but even if I hadn't, there was no possible way for me to make contact with them now. All down the street, the power lines were down, so I knew that there were no communications. I choked back tears, because I had to stay strong for Zach and accept the fact that my parents were already as good as dead.

"You okay?" Trae asked, as he studied my face.

"Yea, fine," I replied.

Before Trae could respond, we heard the familiar whistle again, "Shut up, listen," I said.

Only seconds later, there was a huge explosion. A large fire shot out of the windows of the Recreation Center, which we had just run away from, not even an hour ago. The people inside were dead.

Chapter Six

Because they have never seen anything this devastating before, it took at least five minutes for us to calm Zach and Luke down. Both of the kids were in hysterics. After we calmed them down, Trae broke the silence.

"So, now what? We're alive," he asked. Nobody, except Trae, said anything or could even get another word out. Again, he spoke up, "Well, the way I see it, we can either stay here or fight back."

It turns out that Trae grew up in a military family and he took an interest in weapons defense and survival. He continued, "First, we need to find some weapons, meaning that we should head deep into the city and find a pawn shop or a gun store. But to do that we need transportation."

"I can hotwire a car." I chimed in cheerfully.

Soon, we found a black pick-up truck in a vacant lot. We "borrowed" it and were soon on the highway. There was so much traffic with whoever was still alive in the town. I knew it was like this all over America and I sobbed again. The whole ride, I kept thinking about my parents and crying to myself. I couldn't shake the fact that I would never see them again and that I'd be stuck with Zach, Trae, Marissa, and Luke for the rest of my life.

By the time we reached the city, the streets were empty. There were occasional sirens and explosions; but there were no more gunshots, for now. After about 20 minutes of riding in complete silence, we found a pawnshop. I grabbed a rock and threw it at the window, it immediately shattered and set off an alarm. We crawled inside, trying our best not to cut ourselves on the broken glass. Once inside, we stocked up on everything that would seem to be of use. We found a double barrel shotgun, a Carbine M4, a 9-millimeter pistol, a pair of binoculars, and a knife.

"Take everything you can," Trae yelled at us.

"Got it!" Marisa replied.

Soon, we crawled back out the same way we got in and piled into the "good old pick-up truck," as Trae referred to it. While driving, he once again broke the silence and said, "Next we need to find a place to sleep."

"Any ideas Mr. Know-it-all?" Marisa retorted with obvious contempt.

Knowing that she was finally getting comfortable enough to talk, Trae just smiled at her response. "Yeah, a nice little cabin in the woods, we'll stay there until we have an idea of what's going on."

"How far away is it?" Zach and I asked at the same time.

"It's probably about an hour or maybe two away," Trae said, looking at a map he found in the glove compartment.

"Well, Luke is already asleep, so I might as well be too," Marisa added.

Soon, everybody was asleep, except me, and of course Trae. I couldn't help asking him why he was so calm.

"Well, my dad's in Iraq and my mom's in the Netherlands for a business trip, so I know they're both okay."

I guess I must have had an attitude, because he knew that I was holding something back, "What about you Mike?" He asked.

I felt a cool tear run down my cheeks and I just chocked out the word, "Dead."

Chapter Seven

"We're here," Trae announced.

We all woke up grumbling, as if asking for five more minutes of precious sleep.

"Oh come on! Don't make me beg you," he repeated. After about 10 minutes of threats, we got up and watched, as he shot the lock barring the gate to the old cottage. Then there was silence, as we walked stealthily to the front door, not knowing what was inside or around the house. There was a muffled scream from inside and we knew to be cautious. I picked the lock to the front door and was greeted with a blow to the chest.

Dazed, I looked up and saw Trae and a dark silhouette fighting it out. I could hear the screams of Marissa and our brothers. The silhouette definitely won the fight and had Trae in a headlock, asking him questions regarding our business.

"We ain't mean ya no harm," Trae managed and the attacker loosened his grip. "We just need a place to stay."

Suddenly, a little girl appeared in the doorway and asked, "Daddy, who's that?"

"Nobody, Melanie, go back inside," retorted her apparent father. The girl obeyed and was soon out of eyesight. He then turned his eyes back on us. I was getting up, as he threatened that if we came in between him and his family, he'd skin us all like squirrels. Then he said, "Come inside, don't be a stranger."

When he turned on the light in the hallway connecting to the small dining room, I got a good look at him. E was a white man, in his mid-thirties, with blue eyes, blond hair, and a scar hanging from his eyes to his cheeks.

By now, Trae was getting a second wind. "Don't even think about it, buck eye," the man said with a deep Southern accent. "I got a trusty knife on my hip and another one in my shoe, just in case I need it."

"If you were smart, you'd sit down," I advised.

"Listen to your friend and sit down, cuz it'll be a cold day before I die in my own house with my family," chimed in that familiar voice.

Trae did what was best and sat down.

"Name's Buck," said the Southerner with an outstretched hand.

We shook it.

About that time, Melanie came back downstairs asking for water.

"You two wanna have some fun?" Buck asked, as he looked at Zach and Luke.

"Sure," Luke answered sarcastically.

"Follow me," Melanie said, as she smiled and ran upstairs with Zach and Luke on her heels.

"You said you have a wife? Where's she at?" I asked.

"You try'na be disrespectful young'in?" Buck asked with a little anger in his voice.

"No, sir, I'm just asking" I replied as I got behind Trae, wishing I had brought the guns inside.

"She's asleep upstairs," he finally said. "Sit down."

We obeyed and attempted to be good guests in his house.

"Y'all know what's goin' on?" Buck asked.

"Not really, all we know is that the Chinese army invaded." Marisa spoke for the first time since we've been here.

"You only know a part of it, missy," Buck said smiling. "Basically, the Chinese found the last of the spies and executed them in public. Then Jinping (the leader of the communist country) decided to invade America in waves.

"How do you know this," I asked.

"Military, I got access to files that you'd not even know about." Buck replied. "You haven't seen the worst of it, soon they'll invade."

"What about the gunshots, riots?" I asked in contempt.

"Bingo."

"So what do you suggest we do?" I asked.

"I don't know yet, but I'll tell you what. Because I don't want to let the human race die, I'll keep in contact with you."

Now we were all puzzled, "How, the power lines are all down from the explosions?" Marisa asked.

"You don't know much about low-key coms, do you, missy?" Buck replied. "Hold on a minute, y'all move and I'll kill ya," Buck said with a smile, as he walked off. A couple of minutes later, he re-entered the room with a basic, old school phone called a SAT-phone. "I'll call you when I got something, you need some supplies?" He asked, as he walked into his kitchen, filling a white pillowcase with canned food and drinks.

"It'll sure help," Trae chimed in.

"Here," Buck handed us the pillowcase. "There's an RV with a full tank in the back, it ain't much but It'll give you more space."

"You're not coming with us?" I asked.

"Nah, I'm a family man and I grew up here. This is where I'm a die."

We all shook hands and gave Buck our heartfelt thanks. After we all piled in the RV, got our weapons, Zach, and Luke, we were on our way. It had to be around midnight, because when we walked out the front door, it was pitch black. Soon, we were on our way though, on our own. Buck's cabin faded into the darkness, as we drove away.

Chapter Eight

"Well, he was a nice guy," I said.

"Yea, I guess," Trae answered. "Marissa, why don't you take our brothers to the back room and go to sleep?"

"Fine with me," she replied, "I'm beat," and she was out like a light, sleeping on the bed with my brother and her brother on top. She looked so peaceful and beautiful when she slept. I probably hadn't noticed before because we barely got any sleep. Then I realized that I haven't had any sleep either. So I grabbed a blanket from one of the cabinets and retired on the couch. Maybe when I wake up this will all be a dream. I sure hope so. Despite the jolting from Trae hitting potholes, caused by the explosions, I was asleep in less than five minutes. I drifted away into my own world, at least for a while. Until I woke up to a start.

Chapter Nine

I woke to the booming sound of airplanes and explosions. Trae was driving extremely fast and I had to grab onto the cabinets, and anything else I could get my hands on, to keep my balance. I opened the tiny blinds of the RV and batted my eyes, as I adjusted to the bright sun. There were hundreds, maybe thousands of airplanes. I grabbed the binoculars from the cabinet of the RV and saw what looked to be tiny paratroopers. A couple of miles behind us was a speeding SUV, I decided not to tell anyone because I didn't know if it was the military, or innocent civilians like us just trying to get away. Trae swerved while trying not to hit an enemy Chinaman, who had parachuted onto the little country road that we were taking to get out of the state. I heard a bump and crying in the back room and guessed somebody had probably hit their head after falling off the bed. "Get the guns," yelled Trae, as he looked straight ahead.

"On it," I yelled back, searching frantically in the chest I found near the back room, where everybody else had been sleeping. The first gun that I picked up was an M4 Carbine. When I returned to the window, we were driving through a cornfield and I couldn't see anything to either side of us.

When we emerged from the cornfield, we must have been within range because we were greeted by multiple sprays of bullets. I heard a scream and a bump in the back room and then I broke the window.

"Michael!" I heard a yell from the back room.

"Hold on!" I yelled back. Then I then poked the rifle out the window, as Trae drove as fast as the 27,000-pound vehicle could go, and I squeezed the trigger.

This was my first time to ever discharge a weapon and the kick of the rifle threw me backwards. I got back up though and repeatedly "sprayed and prayed." Glass shattered, as I was grazed by one of the bullets and decided it was time for me to quit.

Soon though, we were out of range again and the shooting ceased. Relived, I went to the back room to find an appalling sight, Luke was shot. He was dead and there were bullet holes throughout the room, everywhere, hundreds of bullet holes in every possible place in the RV. Zach was in the corner sobbing. The RV came to an abrupt stop and Trae walked through the doorway. He was swearing under his breath and holding back a tear, while attempting to comfort Marisa.

"He's dead," she stammered. "He didn't take cover and just like that, he was dead."

Nobody could say anything so we all just silently prayed. Then Trae and I carried his body out of the RV and gently placed him on the side of the road. Zach found some flowers and put them on and around his body. Marisa was the last to get back on the bus. She was clearly the most affected. Although we all just saw him as another "comrade," he was her brother. Marisa had known him for eight years and in a matter of seconds, he was gone.

Chapter Ten

We rode through the night until we saw a dirt road to the right of us. None of us got a full night's rest so we covered the RV in mud to camouflage it and rested. By morning, we were all starving. I opened up some canned beef stew, and separated it into fourths. "When's Buck gunna call," Marisa asked.

"Don't know," Trae said, "he might not call at all, but I do know that since Mike here used all of the ammo for the M4, we're gunna need some more. We can't survive off of a shotgun and pistol."

"What are we gunna do?" I asked.

"Go get the map in the glove compartment," Trae commanded.

I did what I was told and soon returned holding a folded map and handed it to him.

After studying the map, he said, "There's a small town a couple miles away, we're in the country, so there might be a gun store and a small Mini-Mart. We'll stock up, and then get on I-95. It's dawn, so we should be there by 10:00. Does that sound okay to you?"

"Perfect," said Marisa.

Then we got back in the RV and were off. "Hey, Trae," I said, "where do you think everybody is?"

"Either dead, or just like us, try'na survive," he answered.

I raised my eyebrow to his response. "What if there's another place for the survivors to go to?"

This thought intrigued him. "Well, I'd like to know where...."

We rode on in silence for about 30 minutes. Ahead, I could see a few small buildings and one large one. However, the roadblock that was up ahead of us wasn't on the map.

"Look, Trae said, waving the rest of us to the front seat. From the windshield, I saw two small jeeps, a tollbooth, and some armed soldiers. "Take the wheel, drive slowly and calmly, and follow my lead," he said, as he went to the back room. By now, we were stopped at the tollbooth and were being asked questions in a language that I couldn't understand (I figured it was Chinese). When I didn't respond, the soldier got upset and yelled in my face. Soon, I heard two loud, ear gouging, noises and watched as the three soldiers dropped to the ground.

"Dude, what's your problem?" I yelled at Trae, as he was grabbing the weapons and a walkie-talkie that one of the soldiers was carrying.

"Can't do nothing about them now, leave em' here to rot," he said, as he climbed in using the door. He took the wheel again and we cautiously drove up to one of the small Mini-Marts.

"Keep the thing running, there's an extra can of gasoline in the back along with the spare. If we are longer than 10 minutes, you leave. Understand?" I asked, while grabbing the pistol.

Marisa and Zach just nodded in agreement and I knew that they were in shock from what had just happened.

Then Trae and I walked up to the store. The door was unlocked and we heard a shuffling noise from one of the three isles of the store. Trae took out the shotgun and searched the area military style. At the last aisle, there was a boy, who couldn't have been over 14 years old, dressed in all black. He was mumbling something under his breath, while stuffing toiletries into a duffle bag. I guess he didn't see us.

"What you doing with that stuff, kid?" Trae asked.

He jumped from surprise, looked at us, and then went back to stuffing his bag. "Minding my own business," he answered, "and I suggest you do the same."

Trae just smiled and took a step closer. "Whose gunna make me?"

At this, the boy got up and ran at Trae. He was greeted by a sucker punch to the jaw. I just stood there in amazement and watched. Trae had him in a chokehold, but his slender body wormed its way out. I was tempted to grab the pistol and kill him but I couldn't get a clear shot at him. The instant Trae had him in a full-Nelson, I squeezed the trigger. This time, I wasn't thrown back by recoil. The boy looked down to his blood-stained shirt, and fell to the floor.

In rushed Marisa and Zach. "What happened? I heard a gunshot and thought..." She stammered.

"It's okay, I shot him," I said blankly and with relief.

"Why did you do that?" She yelled.

"He attacked Trae," I reasoned.

"You didn't have to kill him!" She yelled. "And why are you talking in this melancholy tone?" She asked, her voice wasn't as high as it had been, so I figured she was calming down.

Zach didn't say a word; he just stared at the lump, motionless body that lay before him. He had rarely spoken since the invasion. As we piled into the RV with the boy's duffel bag, I wondered how Zach was taking all of these deaths. Then, as soon as we turned on the engine, I heard a familiar siren and saw a camouflaged jeep speeding toward us. We pulled off in time for the jeep to catch up.

Once again, I heard the foreign Chinese language through a megaphone. After that, I heard the now familiar sound of gunshots. The back window shattered and I took the pistol and repeatedly shot back. I heard the skid of tires, the smell of rubber and then a crash.

The RV stopped and then went into reverse until we got to the site of the accident. I had apparently shot the tires and the driver was killed in the crash. The passenger was severely injured and crawled out. Trae raised his gun but I stopped him. "I got this," I said and shot the already crippled body twice in the chest. By now, I was used to the sight of blood and the thought of killing. Ding, the same routine as before, we raided the soldiers for their weapons and ammo. I found two hand grenades and was thankful that the pin wasn't pulled. By now, it was dusk, and I decided to sit down on the makeshift couch, which was the only thing in the RV that didn't have bullet holes, and count up the bodies since we left Hinesville. Six... Six dead in a total of three days. Three soldiers at the tollbooth, one paratrooper, Luke, and the boy at the Mini-Mart. I was depressed at the thought of seeing Luke's body, laid out in the back. It was too depressing and I began to wonder what would happen to me, or why death no longer affected me. It was probably because of my parents. I closed my eyes for what seemed like a second and I dozed off.

Chapter Eleven

When I woke up, we were pulled over and it was early morning. Marisa and Zach were still asleep and Trae was missing. I wiped my eyes and took a step outside. I found Trae by the gas tank, exchanging fuel. "Morning' sunshine," he said smiling.

I yawned, "How long have I been out?"

"Long enough for us to get to Raleigh," he kept smiling.

"Well, is there a place for us to get some new clothes and a shower?" I asked and showed him my dirty tee shirt, as an example.

"Yea, kiddo, that's a good idea, you stink," he said, "I just didn't wanna tell you."

He'd never called me "kiddo" before, so I figured it was a step up from what he called me when I first met him. By now, Marisa was awake and so was Zach.

"Where are we?" She asked.

"North Carolina," I answered, "we're heading into the city, but not for long. Just long enough for us to get clean, and probably get a new vehicle because this RV is old, filled with bullet holes, and probably recognized by every soldier within a 50 mile radius."

"Okay," she said unwillingly, "but we should go in shifts."

At that point, Trae spoke up and said, "Me and Mike'll go in first, then we'll come back and tell y'all if it's okay."

By now, we expected a tollbooth. As usual, I took the wheel and got yelled at until Trae shot the people there. Marisa was also getting used to death. She just let out a squeal instead of screaming and yelling. As we rode through the city, we saw a gym. "Maybe there's a locker room, and there should be a shower too," I said as we pulled up.

Trae and I walked in silence toward the gym. The sign that displayed the name was covered in bullet holes. Since the window had already been busted, we crawled inside that way. After about five minutes, we found the shower room. It smelled old and of mildew. However, we figured that it would be better than stinking all day. I turned on the faucet and out came cold but pure water. I took a shower and searched the lockers for dry clothes. I eventually found some athletic shorts and a white tee shirt, about a size too big. Trae did the same and soon we were in the RV, waiting for Marisa to come back. Then Zach. As usual, we were piled in the RV and looking for new transportation. Soon, we came to an empty lot with a car, two military jeeps, and a woman in the process of being arrested.

"Stop," I mumbled, "I said stop!" I yelled a little louder. I guess the bass that appeared in my voice surprised Trae and he pulled over. Now the soldiers were threatening to shoot the woman, as she cried. I pulled up my pistol and without thinking, I shot. As the body dropped, for some reason, time slowed. I heard a siren rise and saw the "helpless" lady run off, as the siren continued to wail. We could see now that the so-called "soldiers" were just dummies, and I knew that we were trapped. Trapped because of me. I sprinted back to the RV, and before Trae could step on the gas pedal, we were surrounded.

Chapter Twelve

There were three military jeeps; two Chinese soldiers came out of each of them. One ran up to the door of the RV and shot the bolt that locked it. He made a grab for Trae first, since he was the closest. I remembered the rifle that we took from the other soldiers and ran to grab it.

"SHOOT!" Trae yelled at me.

When I did, I underestimated how much it would shoot. The entire windshield was shattered. When the soldier's body fell back, the remaining five opened fire. After a bucket grazed my left arm, I remembered a grenade that I took from the crashed jeep. I rushed to the back to make sure Marisa was lying face down, and grabbed the grenade. I opened the window, pulled the pin, and held my breath. Around 15 seconds later, a vehicle erupted in an explosion. Two bodies were engulfed in flames, as I emptied the magazine. Trae then grabbed his trusty shotgun and shot the remaining soldiers. The RV was completely trashed. The engine was beyond repair and every inch of the vehicle was covered in bullet holes. We looked around, desperate for a new means of transportation. As I turned around, I saw the small car that the woman had driven. Thankful for this stroke of luck, we raced to the car.

Earlier, I hadn't noticed how ugly and small the car really was. It was a 4-door car and was a shade of green that I couldn't describe if I tried. It was a major downgrade from our former spacious vehicle, but we'd have to make it work. I took one last look at the once apocalyptic city of Raleigh, North Carolina. I would never believe that the city had once been so busy. So filled with inhabitants. Now it was a barren wasteland of buildings and oppressors.

We then filled the trunk with whatever we could. We had our weapons, the map of the East coast, some canned food, and of course, the SAT phone. Trae drove, I sat in the passenger seat, and Marisa and my little brother sat in the back seat. "We can't drive forever," Trae said, sounding exhausted.

"We can't get shot at forever either," I said tiredly.

"Surely there's a safe haven around here somewhere in this city." Marisa said convincingly.

"Then it's settled," I said, "we'll find a place and stay there until Buck calls."

"IF he calls," Trae mumbled.

Silent, as was usual with us, we didn't talk any more after that. However, after less than 30 minutes driving, we found a small neighborhood within walking distance from the heart of the city. "We'll stay here until Buck calls," Trae announced.

"Who put you in charge?" I asked boldly.

"Nobody else took charge, so I did." He answered me with the same look in his eyes that he got when he killed someone. "And you ain't gunna do nothing about it."

I balled my fist up, but settled on pushing him. Within seconds, he pushed me back and was ready to fight.

"Calm down!" Zach yelled.

I had forgotten he was there.

"Michael, Zach's right," Marisa reasoned. "And Trae, he's just tired, he didn't mean it."

However, I did mean it. But right when I was about to say something, the SAT phone rang. In excitement, I rushed to answer it, "Buck?" I asked.

"Hey, kid, thank God you ain't dead yet, where are ya?" He asked in a low voice.

"Yeah, I know, and we're in Raleigh." I said happily. "Any news?"

"Oh, yea, I heard from my commander. There's an F.O.B. at Fort Worth in Washington. Best you get there soon. When you do, tell them that Buck sent ya. I'll be there soon, so I'll see you there."

Then, just as quickly as he had called, there was a click, and I knew that he had hung up.

"Well?" Trae said looking at me.

"Pack up, we're going to Washington."

Chapter Thirteen

By now, it was dark. Trae decided to drive without our headlights, so we couldn't be seen. Using the reflection of the moon to light our way, he silently drove down the highway. We frequently hit potholes that must have been created by explosions. Then, out of nowhere, headlights came on behind us. The vehicle sped up and rammed us from behind. Trae swerved in an effort to stay on the road. Reaching down, I grabbed the shotgun. Using the butt, I busted the window. As soon as the window shattered, I came up and shot. I guessed that I must have shot the front bumper because the grill of the car was half off. But the driver continued to pursue us. Trae was having trouble steadying the car and I missed shot after shot. Finally, I took one last shot, but to no avail. I missed again.

"Kill them!" Trae yelled at me.

"I can't, I'm out of ammo," I said unhappily.

At that point, the car rammed us again. Trae was so busy paying attention to me, that he didn't have any control of the car. We flipped over three times. I couldn't hear anything except Zach's scream, as he was tossed around the car, since he was not wearing his seatbelt. When the car finally stopped, I was only half-conscious.

What I had thought was a car turned out to be a black van. Or was that my mind playing tricks on me? Four men in dark clothing hopped out of the van and dragged me and the rest of our group out. I was half dragged and half carried to the back door of the van. Blood rushed from my head and my arm and onto my clothes and the attacker's hands.

I used the last of my energy screaming and kicking in resistance. I saw Trae struggling to get free, but then he was punched in the jaw and immediately subdued. The back doors of the van swung open, and I was thrown inside, followed by Marisa and Trae. As my vision slowly started fading, I looked around, blood was everywhere, and I remembered one thing: Zach. Then I blacked out.

Chapter Fourteen

Suddenly, jumping from my sleep, I awoke in a start. Trae and Marisa were still asleep. I attempted to look at their faces, but couldn't because all of the blood that had rushed from my body had glued me to the cold, hard, and uncomfortable floor of the van. The blood from my head wound had clotted and stopped bleeding though. I didn't know where I was, or where I was going. What I did know, was that my little brother was missing and that I had to find him. I heard a moan from behind me and carefully turned around to see whose it was, "Trae?" I whispered.

I heard another moan and he repeated a little more loudly. "Where are we?" He asked worriedly.

"I don't know," I replied.

"How long have I been out?"

"I don't know," I said tiredly.

At that, Marisa was up and looking at us very calmly. While Trae explained that none of us knew where we were or where we were going, I pressed my head toward the front of the van to try to hear what they were saying. I heard a mixture of Chinese and English. My stomach dropped as if I were on a roller coaster. After about five minutes of me not saying anything, Trae said "Well?"

"It's Chinese, and a little bit of English." I said sorrowfully.

"Great!" Trae yelled, as he slammed against the walls of the van.

At that instant, the brakes came to a slow stop for a couple of seconds. Then, the van drove slowly for a few more seconds and finally it came to a complete stop. The doors swung open again and a Chinese soldier stood there staring blankly at us, "Out," was all he said. Then he herded us to a group of chairs and sat down, leaving enough seats for the three of us.

After we were all seated, I asked, "Where's my brother?"

The soldier just smiled, got up, and walked off. We sat in silence in the dark room; only a small, very dim, light emitted from an overhead fixture. The soldier returned shortly with a handful of files. "Your brother, Mr. Tanning, is missing."

I sat in silence as we were asked questions.

"Are you okay?" Marisa mouthed.

I could only look away. "Where are we?" Trae asked.

The soldier didn't pay attention to Trae, just me. But I was in hysterics. The fact was that my little brother, who wasn't even 10 years old, was missing. "He's alive, calm down," the soldier reasoned.

"Where is he?" I asked between sobs, as I gasped for breath.

The soldier went back to his questions.

"Where are we?" Trae asked again.

Once again, the soldier got back up, as if he didn't even hear Trae, and left the room.

"Hey Mike, you okay?" Trae asked, looking at me.

"No, I'm not fine!" I yelled, "My little brother is missing! How am I supposed to be fine?" I yelled again. Then I remembered Luke, who was dead for a fact? At least there's hope that Zach's alive, but Luke was never coming back. That made me wonder how Marisa could live without her brother. Just then, another person came in the room. I know it wasn't the same person because he was slightly bigger and smelled faintly of blood and musk. As he sat down, the light shone on his face. It was Buck.

Chapter Fifteen

"Why are you here?" Marisa asked.

"Why do you think? Paycheck?" Buck retorted.

"So there is no F.O.B. is there!" I asked.

"Oh yea, there is, but I knew that you wouldn't make it," he smiled.

"You mean it's a trap?" I said simply.

"Basically, yes," he said.

"Where's my brother?" I asked.

"At the F.O.B." Buck retorted, "I knew you'd either get to the F.O.B. or die trying. So there's your challenge, save your brother within the week, or you both die."

Trae and Marisa just stood there, as if waiting on my response. I was oblivious to any and everything around me. Time slowed down as I thought about what I would say. I looked Buck in the eyes and said three words: "I'll be there."

"I'll see you then," Buck said between chuckles.

After that, we were released. We were only given the van that we had been kidnapped in. The fact that we didn't have any weapons or food made me feel very unprepared. All we had was the clothes on our backs, and a vehicle with dried blood in the back.

"Follow that narrow road, and soon you'll be on a highway. If you were smart, you wouldn't take it. There are a lot of bandits down there," said a soldier, as he pointed to a narrow dirt road.

For the next couple of hours, we drove in silence. I had the same blank expression on my face.

"You okay, kid?" Trae asked as he looked back with a worried expression of his own.

"Yea," I mumbled.

"You know we'll get your brother back, right?" Trae asked.

I didn't answer.

Soon, we passed the highway and were on a one-way, narrow, dirt road, similar to the one we were just on. My stomach grumbled and when I remembered that we didn't have any food, I looked at the map, and then the gas tank. I noticed that the gas was lower than my morale.

"I think I see something up the road," I said pointing. Soon enough, we came to a very tiny building, no bigger than a gas station.

"No harm in looking," Trae said, parking the van. There were no objections, so Trae and I walked calmly and quietly up to one of the windows. There was a single shadow moving through the place. I knocked on the door, as Trae stood next to me. There was no answer. I knocked again and pleaded "We're hungry, we don't wanna hurt you." Still, there was no answer. As we turned to walk back to the van, I heard a loud slam. When I turned around, there was no one there, just me, Trae, and a small bag that lay where we just were. Slowly, I walked to the bag, and peeked inside. In it, there were five cans of food and two cans of fruit. "Thank you!" I yelled at the door. When we arrived to the van, Marisa just looked at me holding the small plastic bag with the cans of food.

In the glove compartment, there was a small map, folded up. "I guess everybody has a map these days," I said thankfully, handing the map to Marisa.

"Okay, Fort Worth is about an hour away" she said, looking at the map, "following I-95, it's pretty close."

"Okay, thanks," Trae said, looking out the window.

For days now, all I have seen are trees, death, and the Chinese. I can't believe that just last week, I was talking to my parents. Now, I'm fighting for survival, never to see my parents again. I shut my eyes for what seemed like just a couple seconds, and then somehow we were passing by the White House headed southeast. "This is a little quiet for the capital of the U.S.," I said, "wouldn't this be the very first place that you attack?"

"Unless there's nothing there to attack," Trae said. There was a post-apocalyptic feel to the city. "Where is everyone?" I wondered. I felt like we were somewhere that we were not supposed to be.

Chapter Sixteen

As we pulled up to Fort Worth, my heart dropped. At the gates, there was another van, much like the one that we were in. Buck came out of the back with my brother. In the background, several buildings erupted in flames. Fires erupted everywhere. All planes, helicopters, and vehicles had erupted in flames. Through the windshield, I could see Buck wave me over to him. Very carefully, I, and only I, stepped out and walked over. I made eye contact with Zach and he ran to me and embraced me. Buck clapped in amusement. "Well done, kid," he said.

I stared at him. "Where is everyone?"

He smiled, "Look behind ya' kid, before it was bombed, almost half of the people either escaped into the city or they just left...."

Before he finished his sentence, I was walking away in awe. How could a human being do this? Witness someone kill in cold blood. Then I thought of Zach. My innocent little brother, witnessing two bombings. I couldn't think about that at this point, I had to be strong and survive.

"Hey!" A voice yelled from behind me.

When I turned, Buck stood there holding a pistol and ammunition. He gave it to me, and I went back to the van.

"What'd he say?" Marisa asked, as soon as I got in. But before I opened my mouth, more questions were hurled at me. Trae joined in when he looked down and saw the weapon I was holding. Zach had already sat down in the back seat. I asked Marisa to move to the passenger seat so I could sit next to him and was grateful when she did.

"You okay?" I asked.

He couldn't speak because he was too chocked up. "They died," he said in between sobs.

"How'd u escape anyway?" I asked.

"I ran when you got caught," he said. "They found me like 15 minutes later and brought me here"

"Did they hurt you?" I asked.

Zach turned and showed me a scar that went down to his neck. "I got this when they grabbed me and I fell and hit a tree branch. Then I woke up in a bed and that's all I remember," he said.

"What about the survivors?" Trae asked, keeping his hands on the wheel.

"They all ran," Zach said.

"Where? We might need reinforcements. The three of us just can't survive on our own."

"I don't know! Stop asking me!" Zach yelled.

"Okay! Let's all just calm down. We're all tired, let's get some sleep and figure out what do to tomorrow." I yelled back in frustration. The sun was already down when I looked out the window.

"We're almost outta gas anyway," Trae said. Soon after that, we pulled over and started getting ready to go to sleep. For safety, we decided to sleep in two-hour shifts. Marisa volunteered to take the first shift so I handed her the gun and the other three of us dozed off. It took only seconds for me to fall asleep. I had a disturbing nightmare.

Chapter Seventeen

I woke up in a field by myself. Then I noticed that I had no control over my body. I heard different voices constantly calling my name. For every name, I saw a face. Unflinchingly, I stood and watched, as several ghostly faces walked by me. The most depressing face was my mother's. Her once beautiful hair was clumped together and dirty. "Mom?" I directed the question toward her. Without answering, she stood and looked at me. I witnessed no less than 100 dead souls calling my name and clawing at my skin. It was probably because they haven't felt human flesh since they were killed, I reasoned. "Is this what I have to look forward to?" I asked myself. I felt as if I had left my human body and this was all beyond my imagination. I had gone on to the next life. The next thing I remember, a bright light blinded me. When I regained my vision, my body was frozen. None of my limbs worked; I was only allowed to see. After a couple of seconds, multiple people were looking down on me. Every person was wearing black, a uniform, and a smile on their face. One by one, their lips were moving, so they must have said something. But that's when I realized that those people observing me were all people that I'd killed. Then a dark brown wing swung over me and hindered me from seeing anything at all. I was

accompanied by nothing but complete darkness. I was in a coffin.

Chapter Eighteen

Trae shook me into reality. "Wake up! They're coming!" He yelled. I was oblivious to the siren wailing in the background. Wiping the crust out of my eyes, I got up and started running to keep up with him. Before we could get ourselves hidden behind a building, I saw two fast moving vehicles.

"What about the van?" I yelled loud enough for Trae to hear me over the siren.

"Forget it! It's gone!" He yelled back, still running top speed. I saw Zach running right behind Trae. We ran for blocks, until the siren was out of ear-shot. I looked back and saw a hazy red smoke erupting from behind one of the buildings where we just were. Seconds later, there was a booming explosion, which my guess is came from our van. Just like that, everything was gone, again.

Chapter Nineteen

"Is everyone okay," I asked, regaining my breath.

"NO!" Marisa screamed. "No, we're not okay! Look around us. We're in hell!" She said, choking back tears. "Why are we still alive?" She asked in agony. "There's nothing to live for," she was sobbing hysterically by the time she finished her sentence, "my parents are dead, my brother is dead, why aren't I dead?" She fell to her knees with her face in her palms. Then there was a rustle coming from a bush that no one had noticed.

"Don't shoot!" Yelled the bush.

"Don't worry, even if I wanted to, I couldn't." Trae answered.

Then there was a pair of arms that stretched out from the bush and a teenage boy emerged. He was a small, black boy who couldn't have been over 15 years old. He wore a faded white tee shirt with a pair of baggy blue jeans.

"What's your name?" I asked.

He stared blankly at me and eventually said, "Travis."

"Nice to meet you," I said with an outstretched hand and looked as Trae swatted it away.

Hesitantly, Travis inched over to our group. As he looked down, he saw Marisa and asked, "What's wrong with her?"

In the time it took for us to acknowledge his question, Marisa looked up at him and said, "I'm fine, what's yours?"

We were all shocked at how fast she had retorted with that remark. In fear of her snapping, Trae, Zach, and I kept quiet and watched as he replied. "Nothing," was all he could say.

"Who are you with?" I asked, still staring at him.

"A few people in that building," he said as he pointed to a four story building across the street. "We got scared when we heard the sirens and ran there."

"How many people are there?" Trae asked.

"My mom and my dad. You hungry?" He asked, noticing that I was holding my stomach, as it ached and growled.

"Yes," I mumbled and we followed Travis to a small, square shaped room that contained two other people. The man couldn't have been over 40 and the woman was about the same.

"Mom, Dad?" Travis asked. His voice echoed through the small empty room.

"Come in, son," said a deep voice that also echoed through the room.

"I have some friends, can they come in?" He said questioningly.

There was a long pause, and then a feminine voice spoke up and answered, "Sure."

As we walked through the door, to my right I could see three weapons together, they looked like a big, dark colored bundle of sticks. To my right, I saw three chairs, two of them were occupied by the parents. "Hey, dad," Travis said with a smile as he kissed his mother on the cheek.

"Hey T," his dad said, "who are your friends?"

Then his expression went cold, his face turned red as if he was straining himself to remember what our names were. "Umm, actually, I don't know," he said.

"How do you not know their names?" His mom asked.

Then I broke in, "Hi, my name is Michael Tanning," I said with a smile, as if I'm not trying to come off offensive or disrespectful (which I'm not). "And this is Trae, and this is Marisa," I said still smiling.

"Nice to meet you," Marisa said, as she bowed respectfully.

"Travis, may we see you for a second?" His mother asked with a worried look on her face.

"Yes, ma'am," he said.

"Could you wait a second outside?" Said the male voice. Quietly, we walked outside.

"Okay, here's our chance," Trae said. Marisa and I both raised an eyebrow at the look of excitement on his face. "To answer your question, they have guns and food in there," he said impatiently. "We can take it now and there's bound to be a car somewhere around here...."

Then I remembered my nightmare. "No," I said before Trae could even finish his sentence.

"What," he asked. The expression on his face changed from ecstatic to angry in a matter of seconds.

"I'm not killing anymore people," I said firmly, "no more."

She didn't say anything, but Marisa nodded in agreement.

"Fine," Trae threw his hands up in exasperation, "if I have a gun to my head, I blame you," he said gritting his teeth.

Just then, the door swung open and out came Travis. "You can come in now," he said nervously.

We all filed into the center of the room and stood. "What do y'all want?" The father asked.

"We're just trying to survive," I said, "and maybe a little help."

"Speaking of help," Marisa chimed in, "where's the government, or even the president?"

There was another long pause, as if we could hear a pen drop across the street. "The president is dead," the father said. Then all three of our faces went blank. There was a slight squeal coming from my right where Marisa was standing. In a way, I felt bad because I realized at that point that I was more focused on feeding myself than I was concerned for the president of our country. My stomach must have been loud, because the mother went across the room and handed me a can of beef stew. I popped the can, closed my eyes, and ate it raw. The thick, cold, substance felt like a gel as it raced down my tongue. While trying not to gag it back up, I passed it to Trae and he passed it to Marisa. A look of disgust fell across both of their faces. Trying to be polite, we all managed a terse but sincere, "Thank you."

"So what are y'all doing here?" The father asked. "Oh by the way, my name's Terrance." He said with a proud expression, as if those were his favorite words to say. "And this is Pam," he said, looking lovingly at his wife.

"Nice to meet you," we all said.

Then Marisa and I looked toward Trae to finish stating our business there. "Um, actually, sir, we don't know what to do, but we figured that if we found help, we could fight back."

"Where are your parents?" Pam asked. I guess that she figured that they were dead by our silence and glassy eyes. She was quiet for the rest of the time.

Trae began to speak again. "So, we're here because we have nowhere else to go and figured that we can either drive them out, or make it hard for them to take over."

Terrance looked a little excited for a quick second, but then masked his expression with a blank face. "And how do you suppose to do that?" He asked.

"Well, hopefully a resistance" Trae said.

Before Terrance could reply, we all heard a familiar siren and a single gunshot. We all ran to the single window to see what happened, and there lay another dead body. On top of him, were what looked to be two soldiers. One had his gun trained on the body, and the other had his gun in the holster. Around the body, there were multiple posters. I squinted my eyes to get a closer look; they were communistic posters. Apparently, one of the soldiers spotted us because he pointed at the window, yelled to his partner, and rushed to the radio.

"Go!" Yelled Terrance.

Trae, Marisa, and I were at the door watching Travis. "Mom, Dad!" He yelled. "They're coming!"

Terrance yelled, shoving an assault rifle in his hands, and pushed him out to us. "Take care of him," were his last words before the door closed. And Travis was never see to see his parents again either.

As we came through the back door that led to an empty dark alley, five more cars pulled up in the front. Out of them, came heavily armed men that filed into the building. We had to half drag, half pull, Travis past the building when the gunfire erupted.

"No!" He screamed as I clamped my hands over his mouth to muffle his screams. When the gunshots ceased, we knew that the Chinese had killed Terrance and Pam. Like the rest of us, Travis was now an orphan. Actually, none of us know about Marisa's parents. However, I was too scared to ask her. We wandered around the city for hours, until the sun went from a bright, orange red to a small, yellow glimmer behind one of the buildings.

"It's getting dark, we should find a place to sleep," I said worriedly. Everyone nodded and agreed, except Travis, who just gazed around blankly at everything.

"Where can we sleep?" Marisa asked after several minutes of silence.

"Just up there," Travis pointed to a narrow alley between two brick buildings. "The darkness will keep us covered, so we don't have to sleep in shifts."

"Fine with me," I said yawning. Before I knew it, we were curled in a ball for warmth. The cold dirt mixed with the rubble from multiple explosions sent a shiver down my spine. But none of us cared. As soon as we shut our eyes, we were all drifting off to sleep.

However, Travis said something that had me so excited, I couldn't sleep: "In the morning, I'll tell you where the survivors are.

Chapter Twenty

Again, I was haunted by visions of more dead bodies. This time, people I haven't even killed. Countless dead bodies, just walking past me. Their ghostly figures just barely visible. Faces that belonged to people of all ages, sizes, and races. From children to elders, with the same face that they had when they were killed. Some had their eyes and mouths open to a bizarre extent, probably from screams. Some had their eyes closed shut, because they couldn't bear to see the tragedy. Then there was a bright flash, and I appeared in front of a wall. No matter how hard I tried to move, I was motionless and invisible. Along the wall, no less than 50 poor, innocent civilians were lined up. Ten yards behind them, were two Chinese soldiers holding machine guns. There was whispering between the two soldiers, then yelling at the civilians. Seconds later, there were hundreds of gunshots. I had no control of my body and I had to watch the bloody massacre. When the firing ceased, all of the once terrified but living bodies, were laying around lifeless. Then I woke up. There were loud shouts coming from down the street. I rushed over to wake everybody else but I noticed that they were right behind me, running as fast as I was. The light from the early sun lit our way as we weaved behind the buildings of the city.

"Hurry!" I yelled behind me as I heard more gunshots and yet another explosion. I found a small door and nudged it open. We all filed in and clamped our mouths shut to be sure that we didn't make any noise at all. We heard rushing footsteps on the other side. Then there were more footsteps and even more yelling and gunshots. When the noise died down, since I was closest to the door, I peeked my head out to see what trouble awaited us. The alley was eerie and quiet so I interpreted that to be a positive sign. As we cautiously eased our way to the streets, I motioned for everyone to be quiet. It was then that I laid my eyes on the gruesome, multitude of dead bodies that lay before us.

"I'm guessing that there was a riot," Trae said.

We all heard a faint whisper and strained our ears to hear. We turned, to see a man, lying on his back.